Desert Song

by Tony Johnston
Illustrations by Ed Young

Sierra Club Books for Children
San Francisco

Text copyright © 2000 by Tony Johnston
Illustrations copyright © 2000 by Ed Young

First Paperback Edition 2010

Published by Sierra Club Books for Children
85 Second Street, San Francisco, California 94105

Published in conjunction with Gibbs Smith, Publisher
P.O. Box 667, Layton, Utah 84041

SIERRA CLUB, SIERRA CLUB BOOKS, and the Sierra Club design logos
are registered trademarks of the Sierra Club.

Library of Congress Cataloging-in-Publication Data

Johnston, Tony.
    Desert song / by Tony Johnston; illustrations by Ed Young.
—1st ed.
        p. cm.
    Summary: As the heat of the desert day fades into night,
various nocturnal animals, including bats, coyotes, and
snakes, venture out to find food.
    ISBN 978-1-57805-171-7 (alk. paper)
    1. Desert animals Juvenile fiction. [1. Desert animals
Fiction. 2. Bats Fiction.] 1. Young, Ed, ill. II. Title.
PZ10.3.J715De 2000
[E] — dc21   99-36886

Art direction by Nanette Stevenson
Title lettering by David Gatti

Manufactured in Shenzen, China, in March 2010
by Toppan Printing Company (SZ)

14 13 12 11 10
10 9 8 7 6 5 4 3 2 1

For Ann Bustard,
who shared Austin's bats with me
— T.J.

For French Conway,
a friend and a naturalist
— E.Y.

Day is done.
Twilight comes.
The sun goes down
and streaks the clouds
with flame.

The melting heat
is gone.
It leaves
its last warm breath
wavering
over the land.

A quail calls
from a shaded hiding place.

Day is done.
Twilight comes.

Suddenly
with a rush of wings
bats spill from a cave
in a hill.

They have been sleeping
all day long.
Now they pour
into the night
like dry leaves
blowing,
like shadows
on the wing.

They soar.
They race
across the silent sweep of sand,
their small mouse faces
thrust into the wind.

Everywhere
deepening night
is full of insects flying
or creeping
along the ground —
moths and ants,
weevils,
beetles —
seeking the saguaro's
sweet fruit.

Whirrrrrrrr.

Everywhere
the air is full of bats
squeaking,
seeking
insects to eat.

They dip their wings
like swallows
swooping low.

And they hunt.

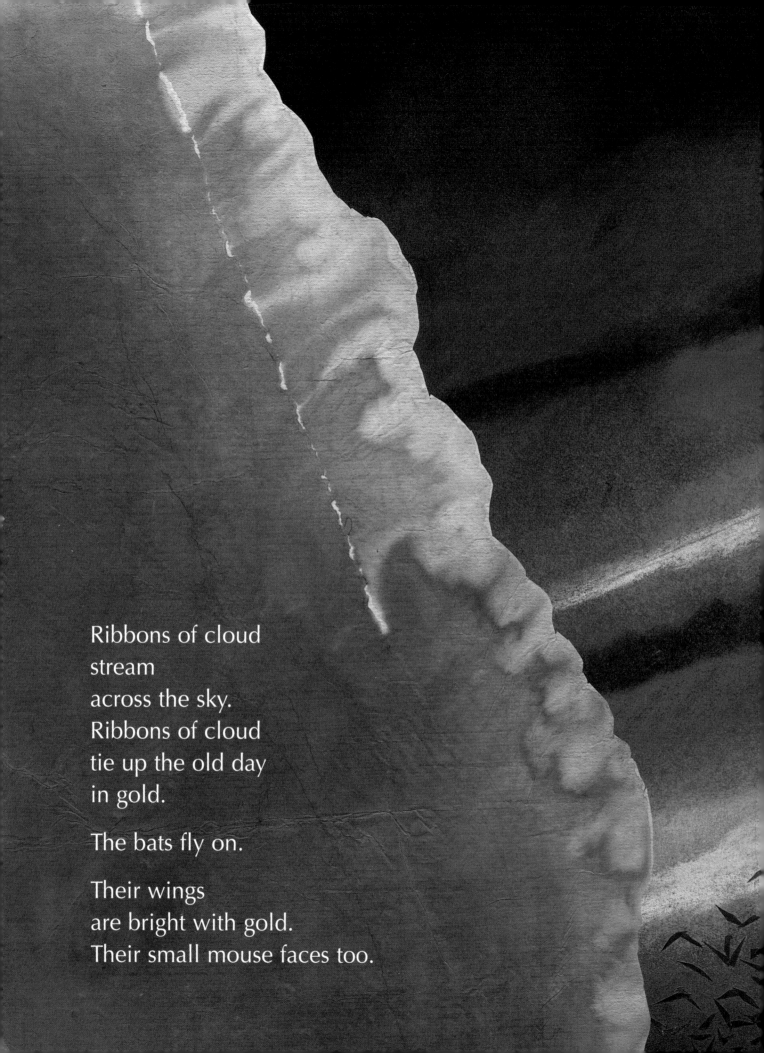

Ribbons of cloud
stream
across the sky.
Ribbons of cloud
tie up the old day
in gold.

The bats fly on.

Their wings
are bright with gold.
Their small mouse faces too.

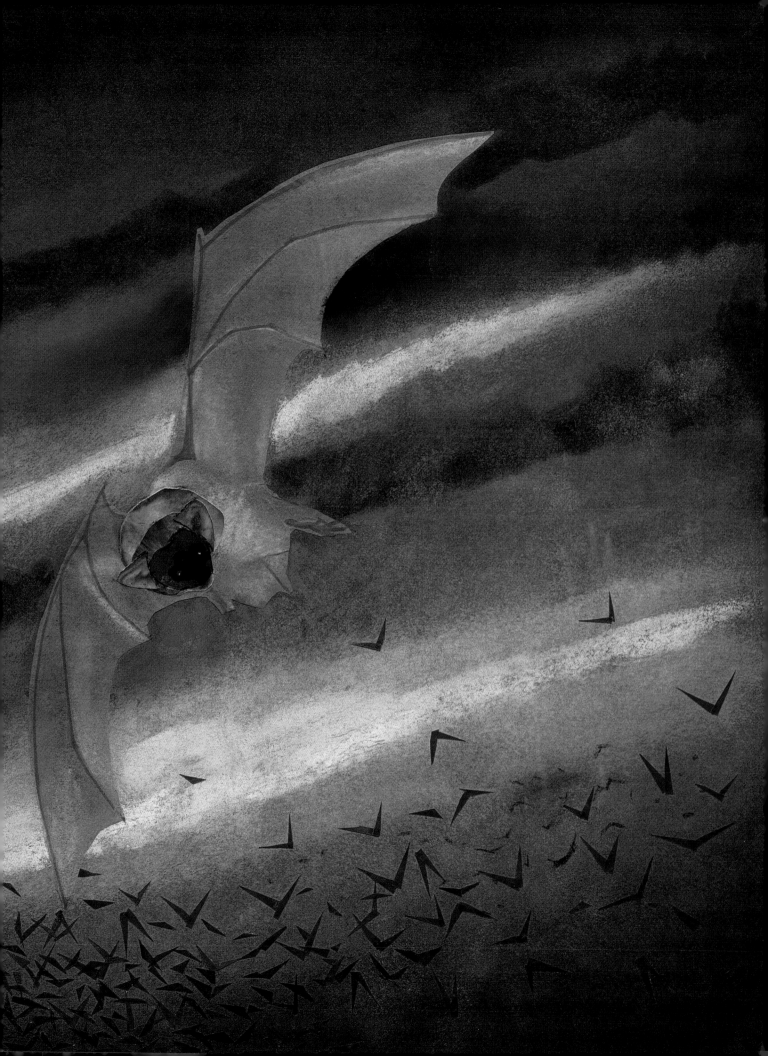

The wind whispers.
Wings whisper
as insects fly through the night,
and the bats fly
hunting them

under countless stars,
along wrinkled hills,
over the desert
sharp with spikes
and spines
and prongs.

The desert fills
with songs.

From a scrawny plant
an owl hoots
one kind of song
as it hunts.

A coyote hunts too.
He prowls
among the spines and prongs.
Then he stops to sing
to the moon.

Song of wonder.
Song of hunger.
Song of being alone.

A pale, cold ribbon of moon,
a snake,
leaves a trail
in the sand
as he slides along.
Silence is his song.

Now one star
in the thinning dark
still glows.

Now morning blooms.

Now many flowers open.
Now many flowers close.

Night things
slip into the cool
of desert hiding places.
They slip into pools of shade,
coyote
and owl
and snake.

As nighttime insects disappear,
the bats fly home
across the silent sweep of sand.

Home to the darkness,
home to their hungry young,
home to a cave
in a hill.

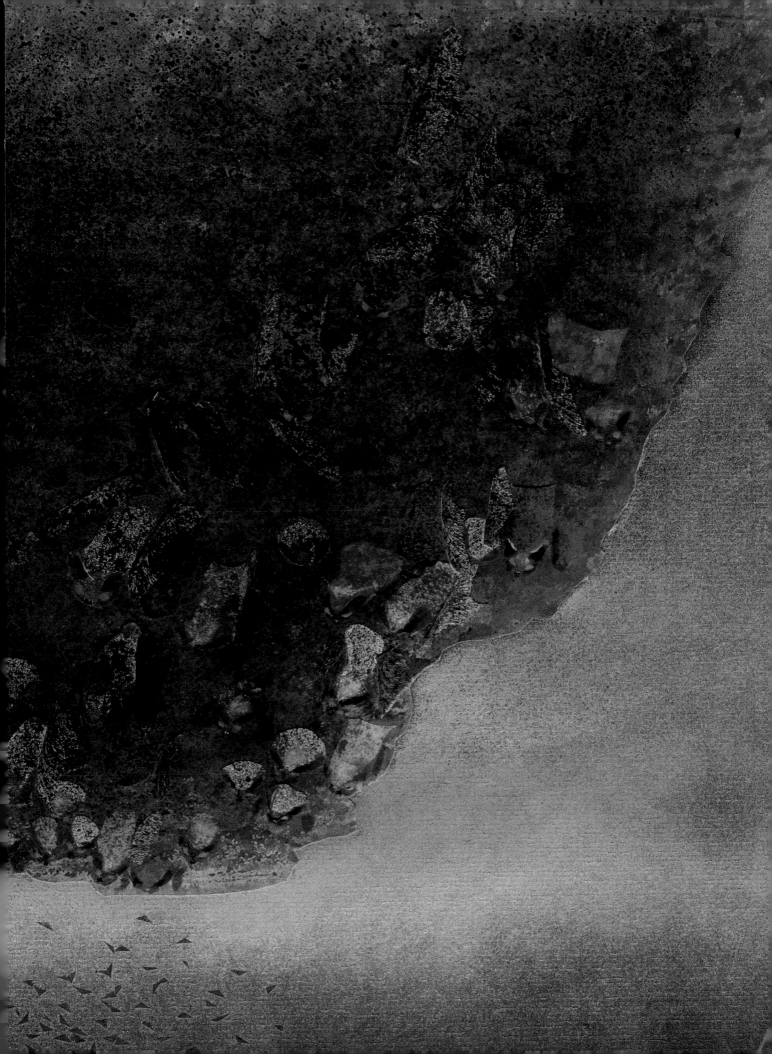

They sleep then,
clustered
close and still,
until day is done
and the sun goes down
and twilight comes again.